Amy's Light

Written and Illustrated by Robert Nutt

DAWN PUBLICATIONS

For you Cindy.

————————

Copyright © 2010 Robert Nutt

The author and publisher wish to thank the following people for their help
in presenting accurate information about fireflies: Louis Sorkin, entomologist at the
American Museum of Natural History; Marc Branham, assistant professor
at the University of Florida; and Don Salvatore, science educator
at the Museum of Science, Boston.

A Sharing Nature With Children Book

Library of Congress Cataloging-in-Publication Data
Nutt, Robert.
 Amy's light / by Robert Nutt. -- 1st ed.
    p. cm. -- (A sharing nature with children book)
 Summary: A young girl discovers a light in nature that
helps her overcome her fear of the dark. Includes an
author's note about fireflies.
 ISBN 978-1-58469-128-0 (hardback) -- ISBN 978-1-58469-129-7 (pbk.)
[1. Stories in rhyme. 2. Fireflies--Fiction. 3. Fear of the dark--Fiction.]
I. Title.
 PZ8.3.N9386Am 2010
 [E]--dc22
                                                    2009038542

Manufactured by Regent Publishing Services, Hong Kong,
Printed January, 2010, in ShenZhen, Guangdong, China
10 9 8 7 6 5 4 3 2 1
First Edition

DAWN PUBLICATIONS
12402 Bitney Springs Road
Nevada City, CA 95959
530-274-7775
nature@dawnpub.com

It was a time of innocence.

A time of "kick the can" and climbing trees,

of riding bikes and skinning knees,

of endless days and porch swing nights,

watching flickering dancing lights.

It was a time to remember.

It happened one night

from nowhere in sight,

by a house near the park,

when everything was dark.

In bed where she lay,

Amy wished it were day.

For the shadows on the wall

were at least twenty feet tall.

When suddenly there shone

a strange light at her feet—

from the curtains, from the window,

from the sky, from the street!

She jumped up and rushed

to the window to see

the most beautiful starlight,

dancing and free.

She smiled to herself

at the thought in her head,

then gathered her slippers

and robe by the bed.

Amy ran down the stairs

through a hall to a door,

where she reached for a jar

that she'd opened before.

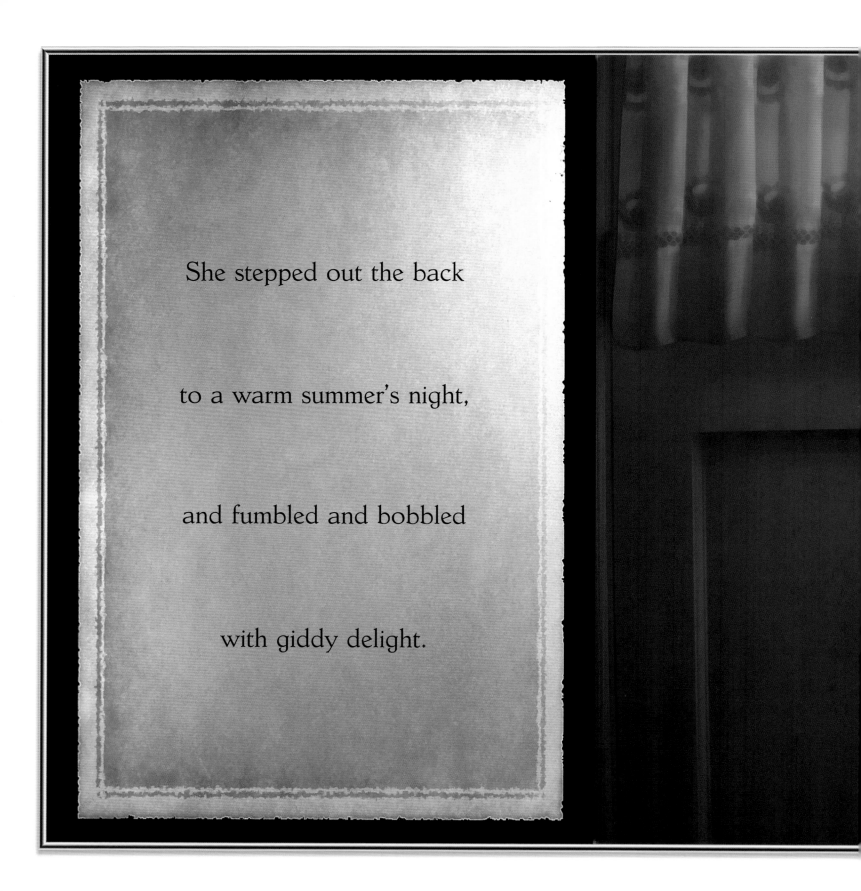

She stepped out the back

to a warm summer's night,

and fumbled and bobbled

with giddy delight.

Out in her yard

such spectacular sights ...

billions and zillions

of flickering lights!

Now she ran, then she jumped,

as she gathered with glee,

first thirteen, then sixteen,

and now twenty-three!

Amy giggled and wiggled

and held up to see,

a warm glowing jar

as bright as could be!

With growing excitement

she ran to the house,

through the door, through the hall,

up the stairs like a mouse.

Closing her door

she made not a sound,

for fear that her secret

would surely be found.

She took off her slippers,

dropped her robe to the floor,

to keep out the darkness

from under the door.

With her eyes on the jar,

from the base to the rim,

she was suddenly saddened,

for the light had gone dim.

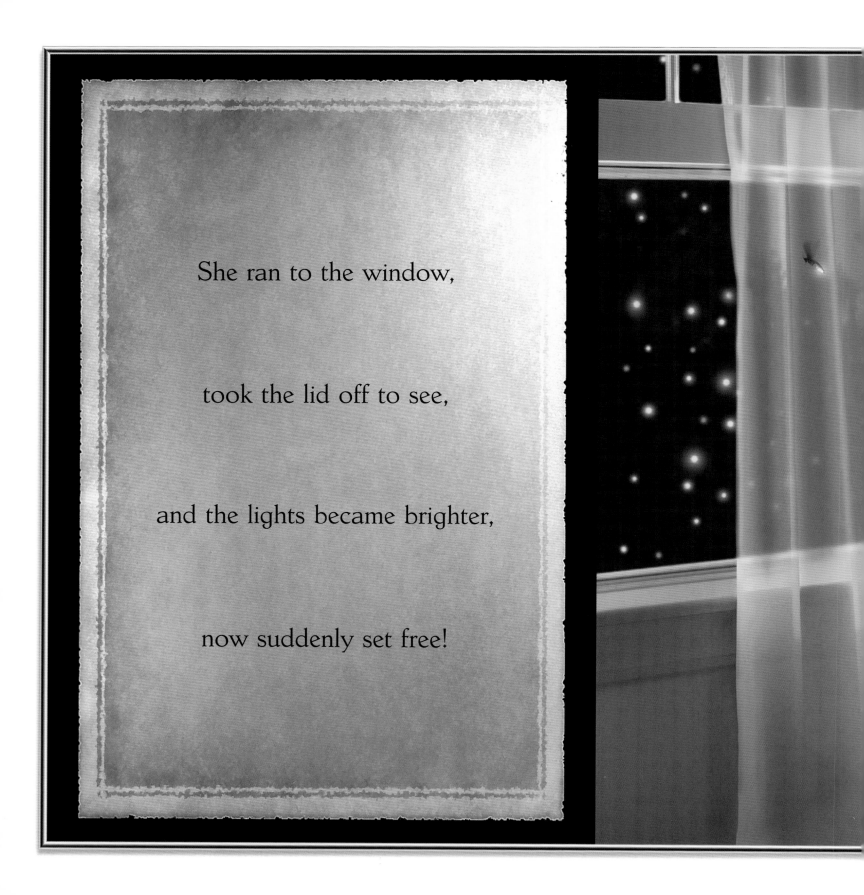

She ran to the window,

took the lid off to see,

and the lights became brighter,

now suddenly set free!

Jumping for joy,

Amy watched with delight

as they flickered and flackered

and flew out of sight.

Dreamily lifting

her robe from the floor,

Amy found that her room

wasn't dark like before ...

and the shadows

on the wall

were really

nothing at all.

Did You Know?

Fireflies, often called "lightning bugs," are tiny miracles of nature. They are a kind of beetle with the innate ability to create light. Fireflies create their magical light, called *bioluminescence*, when chemicals within their abdomen interact. The result is a nearly perfect or "heatless" light. There are over 200 species of fireflies in North America and more than 2000 throughout the world. Each species has a unique style of light. This light is a key to their survival as a group.

In temperate climates, adult female fireflies lay eggs, usually in moist soil, which grow into larvae. Larvae may spend two years underground before they turn into pupae, then emerge as adult fireflies. Each adult firefly lives only a few weeks, just long enough to find a mate and lay eggs, starting the process all over again.

Male and female fireflies of the same species use their distinctive flash of light to communicate. For example, one species commonly known as the "big dipper firefly" will quickly dive just as the flash starts and lift upward to make a J-shaped flash of light. The female waiting on a shrub or in the grass recognizes the flash as a male of the same species. If she likes the look of the male's flash, she will answer with her own. Flash colors of different species range from yellow-green to amber-red.

Most observers think there are fewer fireflies now than in years past. To understand and help protect them, scientists need information. One program that helps scientists is **FIREFLY WATCH**, a program sponsored by the Museum of Science, Boston. At www.mos.org/fireflywatch you can learn to identify fireflies, report on what you find, and have your report posted along with others on an interactive map. The site also tells how to catch fireflies without harming them, and why to let them go soon. Another site, **FIREFLY FILES**, was created by Dr. Marc Branham, a leading entomologist studying fireflies. Go to http://hymfiles.biosci.ohio-state.edu/projects/FFiles/index.html for lots of firefly facts, articles, and links.

A Note from the Author

It was a perfect summer evening at dusk when I caught my first glimpse of what was to become my inspiration. My wife Cindy and I were walking down a peaceful street when we came upon a house with a yard full of dancing, flickering lights. The fireflies were mesmerizing. They seemed to speak to me in their luminous beauty, asking me to share their message, and in that instant I felt a story unfolding.

That night as I lay in bed, the verse just started spilling out of me and I wrote it down. Several times during the creation of the artwork, when my own self-imposed shadows interfered, I was visited by my flickering friends, often at moments when I needed the encouragement to continue. With the continued help from my wife and two daughters, Amy and Christina, I was able to create a story and a message to share the "light" I found.

The joy and beauty of Amy's Light invites us to embrace the delights of nature and find our own light within. I invite you to read the story again and to share your light with the children in your life, and together, make our world a little brighter—one firefly at a time.

It was a perfect summer evening at dusk. Robert Nutt and his wife were walking down a peaceful street in Asheville, North Carolina, listening to crickets, when they came upon a house with a yard full of dancing, flickering lights. At that moment, Robert knew he would write about it. That night, in bed, the verse just started to come—it "just started spilling out of me, and I wrote it down." The light shone so brightly that he knew he had to share it. Robert is also an experienced designer and "self-appointed digital illusionist" who took the photographs of his daughter that form the photo-illustrations for this book. This is his first book.

Thank you for purchasing *Amy's Light*. As a special additional treat, you can enjoy the story in Adobe® Flash® Player format, narrated with charm and delight by the author's eleven-year-old daughter Christina. To download, go to www.dawnpub.com/amys-light and follow the instructions.

OTHER INSPIRING BOOKS ABOUT NATURE FROM DAWN PUBLICATIONS

◆ *Inside All*: takes the reader on a nesting-doll-like journey from the edge of the universe to the heart of a sleepy child, affirming our place in all that is.

◆ *If You Were My Baby*: a "sweet dream bedtime book" for nature lovers of all generations.

◆ *Eliza and the Dragonfly*: almost despite herself, Eliza becomes entranced by the "awful" dragonfly nymph—and before long, both of them are transformed.

◆ *The Dandelion Seed*: the humble dandelion is a fitting symbol of life. Its journey, too, is filled with challenge, wonder, and beauty.

◆ The "John Denver & Kids" series: stunningly illustrated adaptations of some of John Denver's greatest songs (hardback editions come with CD), including *Sunshine On My Shoulders*, *Take Me Home Country Roads*, *Grandma's Feather Bed*, *Ancient Rhymes: A Dolphin Lullaby*, and *For Baby (For Bobbie)*.

Dawn Publications is dedicated to inspiring in children a deeper understanding and appreciation for all life on Earth. You can browse through our titles, download resources for teachers, and order at www.dawnpub.com, or call 800-545-7475.